Running In Plain Sight
&
Other Stories

CHARLES R. BUTTS JR

Running In Plain Sight

Chapter One

It was mid-afternoon on a sweltering and humid summer day. The sun was bearing down and I was weeding the crops when I heard what sounded like gunshots. Scared out of my mind, I ran to the house as fast as I could to see what was going on.

When I reached the doorway, I froze; both Papa and Tully Bates were lying on the floor covered in blood, holding shotguns. Half of Tully's head was blown off, so I knew he was dead. Pa was moaning and trying with all his might to move. Mama, seven months pregnant, was lying on her back near the stove. Her clothes were nearly ripped off, she'd been stabbed a few times and wasn't moving. I'll never forget that far away look she had in her eyes. Tully's son, Buddy, who wasn't much older than me, was standing near the corner holding a blood-covered knife. Enraged, in one

1

motion, I grabbed Pa's shotgun and blew Buddy clean across the room. His blood bathed the floor and quite a bit of him splattered all over the walls. Everything happened so fast. I stood there catching my breath and trembling. I didn't snap out of it until I heard Pa calling out to me.

Covered in blood and gasping for air, he said, "Lee, there's not much time, I need you to listen to me. Run out to the barn, climb up to the loft, look under the second bale of hay and bring me that box." I did what he asked, and when I came back, he said, "Open it up, put all the money in your pocket, and the land deed in the bib of your overalls. Take my hat and boots too, you're going to need them. Mark my x on the back of the deed and give it to Reverend Pope. Tell him I'm donating this land to the church so they can build a school, a separate house of worship and a cemetery. This land's gotta always stay in colored hands, I worked too hard for it. Tell him to bury me and your Ma's bodies here, and to save four or five plots for yourself. When it gets dark, I want you to go down to the rail yard, and sneak on the southbound train headed for Florida."

He continued, "Now go on, get going. I'm sure somebody who heard the shots is probably on their way out here now. You're big for a ten year old, and you have to be a man now. Your Ma and I love you something fierce. You are a product of our love, and no Ma and Pa has ever been more proud than we are. Give me your hand son, and go with God. Take hold of His hand and keep us in your heart always. Be a good man and be strong. Don't start trouble, but don't run from it either. Always be willing to stand your ground and defend yourself. Find work wherever you go and keep moving. You're bigger and stronger than most men, and I believe you can outwork them too. Never stop looking over your shoulder." He smiled, relaxed his calloused grip and passed from this world to the next. With tears in my eyes, and a painful lump in my throat, I put on Pa's hat, slipped on his boots - the first pair of shoes I ever owned, and ran into the woods.

Crouched down and hidden in the woods about a mile away from the farm, and scared out of my mind, I watched the orange sun set before making my way over to Reverend Pope's place. I handed him the deed, along with Pa's instructions. I also told him everything that happened. Short and thin, with kind eyes and a garbled voice, he was extremely grateful for the land. Grateful, but saddened for Ma and Pa, and scared for me at the same time. He and Mrs. Pope covered me, said a prayer for Ma and Pa before he blessed me, anointed my head with oil and sent me on my way. Before sending me on, Mrs. Pope packed some fried chicken and pound cake for me to take along. A bit taller and bigger than her husband - she was really pretty.

Reverend Pope handed me a few dollars and said, "Go with God son, and be forever blessed. I'll do everything your Pa asked me to, and we'll always be praying for you. Find a way to let me know how you're doing from time to time. Your Pa was right, it's not safe for you here. I imagine those boys will turn this town and county upside down looking for you."

Chapter Two

Covering my tracks with pepper to throw off the dogs like Pa taught me, I headed for the rail yard. Knowing I'd pass our farm on the way, I was careful to stay in the woods and out of sight. The night's darkness barely provided cover, due to the full moon and all the stars the sky wore. The aroma of smoke filled the night. I climbed a hill so I could look down on the farm without anyone seeing me.

Larry Boyd and his boys were there holding torches with their hoods off. A huge flaming cross burned in the yard near the front porch. Pat Crane's hounds were sniffing around and howling but were unable to pick up my scent. I heard Larry say, "We gotta find that boy, y'all need to look high and low for him. We're going to kill him real slow and easy. None of 'em can survive if we're taking this land. I'm gonna per-sonally skin him alive too, and let his body swing from this oak all night. The three of them will serve as an example of what happens when you dare to cross a white man. We're going to put them all back in their place. This is the deep south, and down here, white is always right. I swear before it's all over, they'll pay dearly for this. Go squeeze that preacher and see if he knows where the boy is. Load Tully and Buddy's body in the wagon, and then take them to the undertaker before you break the news to Jane. I'll stay here and look around for the boy. Time's wasting, now get going."

I watched them leave with the dogs. When they were out of sight, I ran to the barn, grabbed an axe and crept up right behind 'ol Larry. He'd set the house on fire and was standing back admiring his work while my Ma and Pa's bodies burned inside. When he turned around, I swung the axe as hard as I could at him. It stuck in his chest and he fell backward to the ground. Blood spewed as he gasped for air. I pulled the axe from him and swung hard again, catching him on his legs. With the last blow, I stuck the axe in his head and left it there. Blood covered my clothes and face. Looking around, I drug his body to the porch and into the house. Flames crackled and burned and smoke was everywhere. Since he burned my folks' bodies, I burned his. I'll never forget that surprised look on his face. I'm sure he had no idea he'd burned his last cross, and my face would be the last one he ever saw. Teary-eyed and winded, I grabbed my bag and ran towards the rail yard as fast as I could.

Before long, I made it to the rail yard. I watched the cars hook and unhook with the locomotive. When I spotted a train heading southbound, I made a run for it and hopped into one of the cars. Through the slight crack I left in the door, I watched Attapulgus get smaller and smaller until it was finally out of view.

I imagined an hour or so must have passed before I heard and felt the train slowing down. Fortunately, during the ride I managed to eat something while trying to gather my thoughts. My heart was beating so fast and my adrenaline was flowing like crazy. In a span of a few hours, I'd lost everything I'd known: my folks, our farm and our way of life. Besides the belongings in the sack slung across my shoulder, the only thing I carried in my heart was my folks' memories and the last thing Pa said to me. I was no longer a boy, I had to be a man now. Before the train could slow to a halt, I hopped out and followed the lights, sights and sounds into Tallahassee.

Chapter Three

I wandered around Tallahassee for a few days looking for work and hiding in plain sight at the same time. At night, I slept in the shadows at the rail yards. I kept moving while keeping my head on a swivel. Of course, I missed Ma and Pa terribly and thought about them often, but I knew I had to keep going. A few days later, after I was sure no one was looking for me, I found work in a barn behind a feed and grain store, loading and unloading. I earned sixty cents a week, which was good pay for a ten year old colored boy in 1902. Of course, my boss, Mr. Herman Crump, didn't know that. He thought I was a seventeen year old named Will King from Macon, Georgia.

Tall and thin, with those spectacles always resting on the bridge of his nose, Mr. Crump liked that I worked sunup to sundown without ever complaining. Truth was, I think he took a shine to me, or at least I'd earned his respect. He even let me sleep in the barn's loft. Mrs. Crump would bring me food and books to read in the evening. Short, stout and always smiling, both she and Mr. Crump were kind to me. Before long, he raised my pay to a dollar a week and I saved every dime, along with the money Pa and Reverend Pope gave me earlier.

Months later, one morning when I was on my way into the back of the store, I spotted

Dale Fowler and his boys coming through the front. I heard him tell Mr. and Mrs. Crump that for months they've been looking for a young colored boy who killed two white folks back in Attapulgus this Summer. He said the whole town's been looking everywhere for me and wouldn't rest until my body's swinging from a tree. When he asked Mr. Crump if he'd seen me, he looked him in the eyes and said, "No, I haven't seen him, and he'd better pray that I don't. Seems to me that this boy doesn't know his place and needs to be reminded of it." He even grabbed his rifle from under the counter and cocked it. They shook hands and told him to wire them by telegram if he saw me. They also asked him to deliver me unharmed, because they wanted that pleasure for themselves. When Mr. Crump agreed, they left.

Terrified, I ran back to the barn and hid up in the loft until sundown. I was so scared I couldn't think straight or stop shaking, but despite this, I knew one thing was certain: I'm way too close to Attapulgus, and it's clear those folks weren't ever going to stop looking for me.

Before long, Mr. and Mrs. Crump came in the barn where I was. And because I'd seen him cocking his rifle in agreement with Dale, I didn't know what to think. But my heart was calm, so I trusted it. Ma and Pa always said you can never go wrong following, listening and thinking with your heart.

Mr. Crump whispered it was ok to come down. Once downstairs, Mrs. Crump handed me a plate of food and a glass of lemonade. They wore concerned and horrified looks when I told them what really happened that night, and who and how old I really was. Mrs. Crump had tears in her eyes.

Mr. Crump looked me in the eye and said, "Son, it's no longer safe for you to stay here. I'm sure they'll be coming back if they've even left in the first place. You need to go as far away as possible, California even. Here, take this and put it in your pocket. It's fifty dollars, I wish we had more to give you. Just as you hopped a train to get here, you need to do the same and leave tonight. Stay in the shadows and keep your eyes open." With a firm handshake, he added, "Go with God, son, may He bless and keep you."

Wiping away tears, I said to them both, "Thank you so very much Mr. and Mrs. Crump, I'll never forget y'all and all of the kindness you've shown me."

As I threw my rags and belongings into my bag, Mrs. Crump ran into the house and came back carrying a bible. Handing it to me, she smiled and said, "Take God and His word with you. He and His angels will always watch and keep charge over you. Plus, Mr. Crump and I will always keep you in our prayers!"

"Thank you, Mrs. Crump," I said, "God bless you both. I'm obliged to you both and I promise to keep moving. I'll take God and my faith with me because wherever I go, He'll be there." After a prayer and a hug, I slipped into the night.

Chapter Four

Stowed away in a boxcar headed westward with my fears and wits intact, I began to calm down some. My racing heart was grateful just knowing God was with me. There's no other explanation for me being able to stay a step or two ahead of the folks looking for me. Not to mention the kindness I've been blessed with so far.

Listening to the locomotive's whistle and the soothing rhythm of the wheels meeting the tracks, my thoughts hung on my folks and Mr. and Mrs. Crump. I took the bible from my tow sack and opened it. To my surprise, an envelope fell from it. When I opened it, there was a note from Mrs. Crump. Using the moonlight to see, it read:

Dearest Lee,

Forgive the sloppy penmanship, I wrote this in haste. Here's some more travel money for you. I've saved it for years, and can't imagine a greater cause for it. Take these two hundred dollars and be safe. Mr. Crump didn't even know I had this. We were never blessed with children, but if we had, I would hope they'd be like you. In just a short period of time, you've brought joy to our lives. We know you were raised right by good, God fearing folks. No one, let alone a child, should have to endure what you did. Be safe, and take our love with you always! Being Jewish, it is our custom to render aid to anyone in need. I know you're not Jewish, but someday when you're an adult, I want you to offer kindness and help to another in need. Life is unfair and full of challenges, but you have what it takes to go far! Love always!

Ma and Pa always said there were good white folks and bad white folks in the world, and in these past few months, I've seen and experienced the best and worst of both.

A few nights, and a couple of trains later, I found myself in San Francisco, California. I quickly found a couple of jobs, working on the docks during the days, and washing dishes at a diner in the evenings. I rented a room for two-fifty a week. I saved on food by eating at the diner for free. And of course, minus the toiletries and clothing I needed, I saved the rest.

Taking no chances, I was now eighteen year old Harold Cox from Mobile, Alabama. I was even more cautious, and always looking over my shoulder. I was polite, like I was raised to be, and mostly shy and quiet. Colored folks had more opportunities and were treated a lot better here. Some of them even owned businesses. Like I said earlier, there were a few bad apples, but the good ones far outweighed the bad ones.

In no time, seven years passed and I grew into a man; tall, strong and slender. I have a physique like Pa. Whenever I looked at myself in the mirror, I saw him. I grew a beard just to further mask my identity. Until now, I'd been able to steer clear of trouble, and had earned and saved a heap of money. But the night I headed to the carnival would be my last night in San Francisco.

Like I said, I was a tall and strong young man now. Womenfolk were noticing me, and I was noticing them, but that was about as far as it went. Why take a chance of starting something I knew I couldn't finish. Anyway, I was walking past a bar when I saw a sign in the window announcing an arm wrestling contest and first place was twenty dollars. The night was young and I didn't see a problem with entering it. I easily won every match, setting up the final one against the biggest white man I'd ever seen. Lou Phibbs was 6'6 or 6'7, and was close to three hundred pounds, if not more. He was solid like a mountain. I knew I had a chance because he was pretty drunk, and even more confident. His boys and his pretty girlfriend were there to cheer him on.

We locked hands and went at it. The longer the match lasted, the redder and angrier Lou got. Finally, with one push, I slammed his hand down on the table. The whole bar went quiet, and he was enraged. It didn't help that his boys were razzing him. I suppose the final straw was his girlfriend hugging me. I knew this wasn't good. I took my prize money and got out of there as fast as I could. Lou and his boys followed me out of the bar and up the street, yelling and calling me all kinds of names. I took off running, and made the mistake of turning down a dead end alley. Trapped, all I could think about was what Pa told me about standing my ground.

Lou looked at me and snarled, "Boy, it's one thing for you to luck up and beat me, but it's another to put your hands on my woman! I believe you need to be reminded of your place."

Ella, his woman, was begging Lou and his boys to leave me be. I thought about offering him the prize money, but I remembered I always carried all of my money on me. Growling, he grabbed me and pushed me up against the wall. I managed to get my hand on my knife and plunged it deep into his heart. When he gasped and fell to the ground, I went after his boys. I stabbed one in the back, but the other one got away.

Shocked and screaming, Ella looked at me and said, "Run as fast as you can and as far away as you can get. Lou's folks won't ever stop hunting for you." Soaked in blood, I took off running, heading for the rail yard. There was no need to go back to the boarding house. I snatched some clothes drying on a line behind the laundry house and threw them on. As happy as I'd been in San Francisco, I knew I'd never be able to come back. Trouble had found me and blood was on my hands again.

Chapter Five

Another near death moment survived, but unfortunately two more lives were taken by my hands. I was on the run again, but this time with no particular destination - just far enough for a new start with a new identity. Hopefully, someplace where trouble won't find me.

While running, I spotted a truck leaving a freight yard. I jumped on and hid under the tarp covering its bed. It was freezing cold, and before long, I was numb to the cold air. After a couple of days and nights of riding and hiding, I hopped out in Carson City, Nevada. I wandered around for a day or so, making sure I wasn't followed before finding a clean room and looking for work. Finding work wasn't difficult because I was always willing to take anything. 'All work is good work, as long as it's honest work,' is what Pa always said. I took a job at a ranch mucking stables, another dish washing, and loading and unloading freight on occasion.

Carson City was a great town, and I came to know a lot of good folks. There was a mixture of all kinds: Asian, Mexican, Colored and White folks. It was the first time I ever ran across a whole heap of fair and decent white folk. When I wasn't working, which wasn't often, I studied the Bible, checked out books from the library and read everything I could get

17

my hands on. I still held in my heart everything Pa told me, and was kind to everyone I met. Still saving everything I earned, I could no longer carry it on me. I purchased a satchel to carry my money in.

Just like San Francisco, I got a heap of attention from the womenfolk. It seemed like they were everywhere I turned, and I was no different from any other man. I wanted a family of my own - a wife and kids. But I felt in my heart it wasn't fair to make my troubles someone else's. My life was already at risk, and I knew it wouldn't be right to endanger anyone else. Although, it didn't stop me from having fun. I'm not proud of it, but I slept with a heap of women. But no matter how strong the feelings I had for them grew, I could never commit myself to anyone.

Summers in Carson City's desert climate were blazing hot during the day, and freezing during the night. It was very dry, and it didn't rain too much. Winters were cold, sunny but cold nonetheless. Folks here were friendly and neighborly enough, but mostly they minded their business and kept to themselves. Of course, like anyplace else, Carson City wasn't without its bad apples. Life was good, but I was always waiting for the other shoe to drop.

Chapter Six

Years passed, and the world was changing for the better. With the Great Depression and World War I behind us, things were looking up. As was my habit, I worked, saved and read all I could, and when I wasn't doing these things, the womenfolk kept me pretty busy.

I got good at hiding my money. Hiding it in plain sight like Pa had taught me. No one I'd ever known was better at hiding things than him. Now I'd earned and saved so much money, I had to buy a set of leather saddlebags to go with the satchel I already had. I also kept a change of clothing and some toiletries on me in case I had to leave in a hurry. And of course, I was never without my knife. Carson City was always bubbling with excitement, there was always a lot of activity with folks coming and going at all times. Aside from the women I'd court and call on, I didn't allow myself to get close to anyone. Every moment could be my last. The way I saw it, trouble was always lurking around the corner, hoping for some ill-fated soul to find it.

Time seemed to just fly by. I was now in the back end of my twenties and starting to get a little restless. Carson City had been really good to me. I'd grown into a man, had fun with women and stayed out of trouble for the most part, but now I yearned for a change. I didn't want to stay anywhere too long and get too careless. I'd met a couple of Pullman Porters in passing, and they were sure they could get me a job. The idea of working on a train opposed to sneaking on one excited me. Traveling, working and seeing the country on a train would be ideal. So without saying any goodbyes, I grabbed my money and my things and headed to the train station. Of course, on any trips taken down South, I'd have to be extra careful. Plus, I figured enough time had passed for me to reach out to Reverend Pope, to find out how things were back home and let him know how I've been.

In the wee hours of a crisp, cool autumn morning, I pulled up roots, and boarded a train headed for New York City. Having been hired a month prior, I was excited to begin a new life. So with my hopes, dreams, and money, I made my way to the employee's lounge to learn the ins and outs of my duties on this leg of my journey.

In less than a month, I knew my new job like the back of my hand. I got along with the fellas and minded my business. The routines and routes became as familiar as second nature. Of course, the northern white folks were always better than their southern counterparts. The southern passengers were rude, but they tipped well. Especially when we played up our southern manners: yes sir, yes ma'am, no sir, no ma'am, and 'mo tea or coffee sir or ma'am.

Chapter Seven

My boss, Mr. Henry Pike, was one of the finest men I'd ever been blessed to know. Smart and hardworking, he said he saw a lot of himself in me. Truth be told, I saw a lot of Pa in him. He was a huge, dark man with a deep voice and a warm smile. His wife and two daughters lived in Mobile, Alabama, and on occasion, he'd invite me home with him for worship, fellowship and some good home cooking. His wife, Ms. Odessa, was thin and kind and his daughters, Gail and Fanny were beautiful. Gail, the oldest, was married to a Negro Ballplayer, and the younger one, Fanny, was a school teacher. She played the piano at church, and we could never seem to take our eyes off each other. Mr. Henry knew my skirt chasing ways, 'cause he'd seen me on the road, heh-heh, and I'd seen him too. But out of my deep respect for him and Ms. Odessa, I promised to leave Fanny alone.

Mr. Henry was a great family man and the pillar of the community here in Mobile, and on the road, he was a true hustler and a ladies man. I got to know both sides of him well. I suppose he used his wild side to maintain his home side, if that makes any sense. He was always looking for the next dollar and was willing to do whatever it took to get it. He taught me how to play poker and everything he knew about cards. He showed me how to run hooch along the routes and even set me up with his contacts. New York and Chicago were my favorite cities. The dancing, Big Band Swing music, and the ladies there were better than anyplace else I'd been. Mr. Henry liked being a porter because on the road, he could be who he couldn't be when he was home. On the road, he really let loose and had fun like all of us.

One night in Brooklyn, we were in the back of a speakeasy with two ladies. I was with Shirley Easter, who I saw from time to time, and Mr. Henry was with Pearl Gatling. Now Pearl happened to belong to Bo Collins, the biggest number runner in Brooklyn and wannabe tough guy. And the way Mr. Henry and Ms. Pearl was looking at each other, there had to be some strong feelings between them. Anyway, it wasn't long before Bo and a couple of his boys came busting through the door. He walked right up to our table, pulled back his coat showing his gun, and asked Mr. Henry to step outside so they could talk. Someone like him cared way more about his reputation than any woman. He had lots of women like Ms. Pearl, so she was replaceable to him, but I guess his respect and reputation were not.

When he and Mr. Henry made their way to the door, I stood up to follow them. I sensed trouble; you could feel the tension. One of Bo's boys tried to grab hold of me. Instinctively, I sidestepped him and stuck my blade deep in his chest. He gasped and fell hard to the floor. Shirley broke a champagne bottle across the other one's head, he backhanded her before I stuck him too. He screamed at the sight of his blood squirting from his neck. All hell broke out then, and folks were shuffling and trampling each other trying to get out of there. Covered in their blood, I was almost at the door when a gunshot rang outside. I saw Mr. Henry lying in the street gurgling and trembling in a puddle of his blood. Folks outside said they struggled over the gun, and when they fell to the ground, the gun went off. When I reached him, he had the same faraway look in his eyes that Pa had before he passed on. I'll never forget him taking my hand and saying, "Get me home to Mobile, young fella. Tell Odessa and the girls I love them with all my heart."

"I promise," I replied. He closed his eyes and never opened them again.

We brought his body over to Shirley's and cleaned him up before I made arrangements to bring his body home. When we arrived in Mobile, I lied to Ms. Odessa and said Mr. Henry was shot when a couple of guys robbed us. I saw no need for the truth to hurt them even more - it wasn't going to bring him back. It was a sad time all around. The whole town of Mobile mourned, and Ms. Shirley was wrought with guilt and blame. Mr. Henry was put away with his dignity and honor intact, and his flaws and body were buried on a hill in the church cemetery on a cold and sunny winter day. I suppose the greatest lesson I took from Mr. Henry was 'love is perfect but people aren't.' He was no different than anyone else, and in the end, his heart overruled his head. No one can judge us but God, and if he can forgive us, why can't we? Blood had been shed again, and though it was justified, I had to leave a town I loved and never come back. Being this close to Attapulgus made me want to go there. But even though it's been more than twenty-five years, I decided to just keep on moving. However, I figured it was time to try to reach out to Reverend Pope.

Chapter Eight

Before leaving Mobile, I'd already decided to leave the railroad and head westward to Kansas. But before I did, I met Reverend Pope in Columbia, South Carolina. Neither one of us felt safe meeting anywhere in Georgia. Some of those good 'ol boys had gone to glory, but their sons were just as mean-spirited and no doubt still looking for me too.

It was a mighty fine reunion for us. He brought his son Randy, who would someday succeed him. I was saddened to learn that Sister Pope passed in her sleep ten years earlier. Reverend Pope was older in the body, but his humor and wit were still razor sharp. He still wore his britches pulled high above his waist, and his hair was still slicked and shoe-blacked as ever. He remarked about how much I looked like Pa. Pictures of the church and school made me feel so good, but the pictures of my folk's grave hurt my heart and took me back to the night I lost them. They've been gone a long time, and not a day goes by that I don't miss them. I'll carry them in my heart always.

We agreed to keep in touch, and after telling me how proud my folks must be of me, he told me that he was too. He said if for some reason God calls him home before we meet again, I can always reach out to Randy.

I moved to Topeka, Kansas to start over again. The world was nearing 1950, and its second war was behind us. I suppose the world had changed a little for the better, with the colored soldiers getting a real chance to fight for their country. I hear there were even colored pilots. But I'm sure once they returned to America, they were reminded that much hadn't changed. Colored folks were still beaten and raped, and our bodies still swung from trees and washed ashore from rivers and creeks.

I settled pretty smoothly in Topeka, with a place to lay my head and a couple of jobs. I vowed to steer clear of trouble - it didn't find me, nor did I seek it. The folks were pretty nice, and the white folks were more than cordial. I was nice but fed folks from a long handled spoon. During the period I was there, as usual, my only weakness was women. I courted and called on more than a few of them, but I was always honest with my intentions. Aside from that, the only changes were the seasons and knowing the world's spinning around the sun. What pleased me most was knowing that I was leaving on my own terms. I calmly packed my belongings, and walked toward the bus station before catching a jitney cab and riding the rest of the way.

Chapter Nine

I finished the fifties out west near San Jose. Believe it or not, I'd begun to slow down a little. I was middle aged now and had begun to look and feel every bit of it. Until now, I'd always been strong and healthy as a horse, but I suppose all of the moving and running had begun to take its toll on me. Head colds became harder to shake, and food didn't always stay down. When it did, using the bathroom hurt a lot. I just brushed it off and kept on moving on. Though, in my heart, and in the back of my mind, I knew something wasn't right.

In 1960, I moved to Washington, D.C. - the nation's capital. The country was changing because colored folks were forcing change and demanding to be treated equally. Not solely colored folk, there were a heap of good white folk fighting with us too. In Joe Louis, we had a colored boxing champion, and because of Jackie Robinson, there were colored ballplayers. Schools were now integrated, too. Integration will be great in the long run I suppose, but it hurt a lot of colored business folks. The Negro Leagues, rooming houses, restaurants, dry cleaners and such.

As a whole, though, I suppose it was a good thing. We were marching, boycotting and sitting-in to affect change. In D.C., there were so many colored folks, and I felt comfortable letting my guard down a bit. I must admit, it did my heart a heap of good to be smack dab in the middle of it all. Colored folk began to grab more than a toe hold in every important area: sports, acting, medicine, law and even politics. Wouldn't surprise me if we had a colored president in the White House someday. I'm sure I won't be here to see it, but God willing, some of these young ones will. This country's tangled up in two wars: one on the other side of the world and one here on its own soil for equal and civil rights.

Chapter Ten

The sixties also brought sadness with it. I bore witness to the best and worst of humanity. Bad crimes against colored folks still took place. The country spends billions to put a man on the moon, but turns a blind eye to poor folks of all colors who suffer and live without basic needs and adequate living conditions. I'll never understand how some humans can treat others so callously. Both President Kennedy and his brother were killed, and civil and voting rights acts were signed into law. In 1963, a couple of hundred thousand or more folks marched on the capital for our civil rights. I was so proud to be a part of that- it was a wonderful time. I'd never in my life seen so many colored folks in one place before, wasn't even sure that many existed. This decade also took a couple of great colored leaders away from us - Dr. Martin Luther King Jr., and that Malcolm X fellow. Both filled us with so much hope, and when they were assassinated, great sadness flooded our hearts.

By this time, Reverend Pope had passed, but Randy and I talked often. I wasn't feeling well myself, and had earned and saved a lot of money over the years. By now, though, I'd managed to stash the money in a couple of banks. Just to stay busy, I'd piddle around and find a little day labor when I was feeling up to it, but most of the time, I stayed in my apartment reading and watching TV. Unfortunately, the downside of not having a family of my own means I have no one to pass my wisdom and legacy to. The reality of dying alone saddens me, but I've always believed it was unwise to endanger another life. I have no regrets, actual or imagined - I ran to stay alive and keep the promise Pa swore me to. As far as all the bad I've done, I know God has forgiven me, and I've forgiven myself.

Chapter Eleven

By 1970, I retired for good. I'm a couple of years away from 80 now, and I've slowed down a great deal. At this point of your life, you're just grateful for everything. Grateful to still be above ground, and for every moment the Lord gives you. I've been blessed with nearly four score, and looking back, I realize I didn't get here alone. Besides, God Himself put some wonderful folks in my path. It's kind of funny I suppose. You're wiser the older you get, but physically, all you can do with the wisdom is pass it on somehow and hope it doesn't follow you to the grave.

I suppose my plan now is to squeeze as much life out of the time I have left. I know my health hasn't been good for some time now, so I decided to lay my eyes on some of the places I've read about. I decided it's time to walk on foreign soil.

My money safely stashed away and passport in hand, I made it to my first leg of my international journey: Paris, France. I know traveling while not being in the best of health wasn't too smart, but it's something I had to see in person. The folks were really nice and friendly, and being there was far better than anything I ever read about. When I saw the Eiffel Tower, it was so beautiful that my eyes shimmered with tears. After a couple of weeks, and not feeling any better, I headed off to Italy. I toured Vatican City, vineyards and its beautiful countryside for a couple of more weeks. Traveling and seeing all these wonderful sights made me long for companionship. I wasn't healthy enough for romance, those days were behind me. I was supposed to visit Japan and Egypt next, but I was feeling sicker and too weak to continue my journey. I needed to get home, see a doctor and get in touch with Randy. I know it was foolish to travel in the first place, but Pa used to say, 'there's no dishonor to try and fail, but it's always dishonorable and spineless not to try.' Though I've suffered a lifetime of loneliness, I've known and experienced all kinds of love also. I've learned the most important thing in this world is love, and keeping an open heart is the key to love finding it, filling it and passing it along to another heart.

Chapter Twelve

Back in the states, I decided to move to Atlanta, Georgia. Being only a couple of hours from home felt strange, and tempting to say the least. It's July 4, 1976, the nation's bicentennial birthday as well as my eighty-fourth birthday. My health's fading, but I'm grateful for the journey nonetheless. Aside from my folks being taken away from me, I wouldn't change a single thing. I've made many a mistake and learned many a lesson. But I believe every lesson brings a blessing. Every moment, situation and experience has shaped me into the man I am today - a human being, with faults and flaws like everyone else. Life is funny, and if you keep your eyes and ears open, your heart will reveal and tell you all of its secrets.

Aside from love, the most important thing in life is time. Its passing will go on whether we want it to or not. It never changes, yet it changes everything. It's the only thing in the world we can never get back. You can get money, health, family, career and even love, back, but never time.

As tempting as it was to go to Attapulgus, I kept my wits and stayed put. Like I said earlier, I'm not the picture of health anyhow. Besides, why tempt fate now? My heart tells me the sand is running through my hourglass a little faster these days. But in my heart of hearts, I really want to see home just one more time before that chariot swings low for me.

Chapter Thirteen

I spoke to Randy and he drove up for a visit. I found a nice, high-rise apartment in the West End, and my days were filled with doctor visits, checkers, chess with some of the fellows, puzzles, and TV.

Health wise, I wasn't feeling any worse, nor was I feeling any better either. More and more, blood filled the commode whenever I used it, and it's becoming more and more painful to go. I'm eating less because of the pain I know that comes after. I've dropped some pounds and my clothes are looser. I even felt like crossing the street some Sundays to that little church house with the red door. It was good for my spirit.

It was well into Autumn now, full of crisp, cool mornings, colorful leaves, warm days and cool nights. At this point, I doubt I'll see too many more Autumns, if any at all. I'm neither sad nor afraid, just grateful for the journey. It could have ended that night in 1902, but that wasn't God's plan. Since that night, He's carried me seventy-four more years and I wouldn't change a thing.

Whenever Randy took the time to drive up to check on me, I felt really special. He's the closest thing to family I have left. Reverend and Mrs. Pope did a great job raising him. Had I been blessed with kids, I'd want them to be just like him. A God- fearing man with a good heart, devoted to his family, church, and community. Some of the folks here at the towers never have any visitors. That has to be a lonely feeling. But Randy takes me to order groceries, some appointments and to the pharmacy. He even holds Bible study with us. I get a warm feeling in my heart every time he tells me how Ma and Pa's gift of the land has helped the community.

Chapter Fourteen

I find myself dreaming the same dream nearly every night. I'm ten years old again, sitting at the kitchen table laughing and talking with Ma and Pa. We didn't have much of anything, but our farmhouse was overflowing with love. We were pretty much living hand to mouth with our ends barely meeting, but it was the happiest time of my life. Mama was pregnant, and every night I read to the baby while Pa rubbed her feet. They were certain the baby was a girl. I didn't spend nearly as much time with them as I would have liked, but I believed I took with me the very best they had to give me.

Cancer has overrun my body now. It's in my colon, and my doctor wants to operate or begin radiation before it can spread any further. To be honest, I'm leaning toward neither option. Besides, at eighty-four, who wants to be cut on or even try to endure radiation at my age? I've lived a full life, and my only regret was leaving home and not being able to root myself any place for a long period of time. I'm not afraid to leave this world either. It's funny, I spent a lifetime running all over the country from folks, but I can't outrun cancer - I'm not even going to try. But before it takes me for good, I needed to set my eyes on Attapulgus one last time. If only to visit my folks' grave before this old, tired and ill body is laid in my own. And I can honestly say I don't mind, I'm way too tired to mind at all.

Chapter Fifteen

On the first day of Summer, Randy came up and drove me back to Attapulgus. The blue, cloudless sky, bright sunlight and warm temperatures made the day even more beautiful. I was so excited, I could hardly sit still during the ride down there. The thought of seeing my hometown thrilled me to no end. After running for seventy-four years, I'll never run again.

When we reached the town square, everything looked so different. Paved streets, modern buildings, and shops - but the most glaring difference was seeing white and colored folks laughing and fellowshipping with each other. That in itself brought tears to my eyes - if I don't see anything else while I'm here, that's more than enough. Randy pointed out certain things around town as we drove, and suggested we go to his house and rest a bit before showing me around, and I thought, since I'd waited this long, what's another hour or so?

Randy and his family had a nice, four sided brick home on the outskirts of town. Florence, his beautiful wife and their children, Randy Jr. and Cheryl, were incredibly sweet and kind to me. Their family reminded me of my own. Since it was Wednesday, Randy suggested we head over to the church for Bible study after supper.

When we arrived at the church, the parking lot was full of cars. With the orange setting sun on the horizon, a couple of deacons were directing traffic and coordinating the parking. When we entered the sanctuary, there was a hush before everyone stood and applauded when they saw me. What a wonderful surprise, it made every moment away worthwhile. There was food, drinks, and even a huge cake, but the biggest surprise was the white folks. One of them was Porter Fowler, Dale's grandson and mayor of Attapulgus. After sharing the cake, shaking every man's hand and hugging and kissing every female cheek, Porter stepped up to the podium, grabbed a microphone and called for everyone's attention. Turning to me with tears in his eyes, he said, "Mr. Sills, I think I speak for everyone when I say we're all truly grateful to have you home where you belong. I've carried a message with me for more than fifteen years, and now I'm finally able to give it to you. On his deathbed, my grandfather told me what took place on that tragic night all those years ago. He wanted no part of what happened, but back then either you're with them or against them. And to go against them meant risking your life and the life of your family. He said when he saw you coming in the back of that feed store, he was so happy you'd survived and got away. But because he was with a couple of folks who didn't want you to live, he pretended not to see you and act just as ignorant as the fellows with him. He regretted it for the rest of his life. He prayed for you and vowed to do everything in his power to help colored folks and right some of the wrongs that were done against black folks back then. As everyone here knows, our family's businesses grew and grew. Grandpa's final wish was for me to apologize for him and present this church with a million dollar check donated in your name. It can't begin to undo how you were wronged, but hopefully, you can forgive him someday. Also, along with myself, the town council voted unanimously to rename Main St. to Sills St. And from this day forward, every June 21 will be Leander Sills Jr. day!" The crowd erupted, tears couldn't stop flowing down my cheeks and Porter and his family walked up to me and gave me a huge hug.

Taking the microphone with my trembling hand, I said, "I accept the apology, if God can forgive, I surely can. I learned a long time ago that holding on to hatred and never forgiving only hurts the person who's been wronged. My folks taught me that holding on to anger robs you of your power and dims the light inside of you even more. Thank you for your generous gifts, it's more than I could ever have hoped for." After more applause, we adjourned and everyone went home. I was on such a high, I didn't ever feel like I was ever going to come down from it. My heart was overflowing with so much joy.

Chapter Sixteen

I was lying in bed, replaying over and over what happened at the church earlier, when Randy knocked and stuck his head in to say good night. I motioned for him to turn on the light and come closer - I needed to ask him another favor. Smiling, he said, "Sure thing, Mr. Lee, anything. What can I do for you?"

"Could you bring me those leather satchels from the closet please?" When he brought them over, I asked him to open them for me. The look on his face was priceless. I told him, "There's more than five hundred thousand dollars here, my life's savings. Take twenty thousand of it for seeing after me all of these years, then minus my final expenses, add the rest to the Fowler's donation to create a scholarship fund at the church named for Mary and Leander Sills Sr. Give me your word."

"Not only do you have my word, Mr. Sills, but I refuse to take any of the money for myself. It's an honor and privilege helping you. Daddy always told me stories about you and your folks, about how good you people are."

"Well, my Ma and Pa were truly good, for sure, but as for me, the jury's still out and I've yet to face my judgement. I've taken some lives and I'll have to give an account to the Lord for that. Although it was always in self-defense,

I've forgiven myself, and I'm sure the good Lord has forgiven me too."

"I know. He's forgiven you, sir, because Jesus died for all of our sins."

"Well, thanks again, young fella. I'm sure your Ma and Pa are very proud of you because I sure am. Don't ever stop making us proud."

"I'll do just that, Mr. Lee. Now you get some rest. Good night."

"Good night, son."

Chapter Seventeen

For the next three days, Randy took me all over town and introduced me to practically everyone in town, colored and white. Each afternoon, I had him bring me to Ma and Pa's graves to pay my respects and say a few words to them. It made me feel good, in fact, I felt as if they were there with me, which felt really great.

On Sunday, it looked like the whole town came out to worship. The parking lot, sanctuary, and balcony were all jam packed. Randy is an amazing preacher, and the spirit of the Lord was truly present. During the sermon, I started feeling strange. I felt flush with heat and light headed. Finally, during the prayer before communion, I felt myself slumping over in my seat. The nurses tended to me, and someone called 911.

The strange part of this is that the whole time I felt better than great. I felt lighter and freer than I have in a long time. The paramedics were trying to revive me, Randy and the church were praying for me and I was watching the whole thing unfold before me. I was telling everyone I was ok, but no one seemed to hear me. Then in a flash, I pulled away and watched my body lying on that pew. When I looked at the rear door, I saw Ma and Pa standing and waving at me. That's when I knew I'd passed on from this world to the next. Death had snuck up and taken me. I wasn't afraid and didn't regret a single thing.

Ironically, my home going celebration was held on a hot, humid and sunny June day, similar to the day I ran for my life. The whole town came out to show their respects. Afterwards, my body was lowered into the red clay dirt alongside Ma and Pa. The frightened boy who ran away so long ago no longer had to look over his shoulder. I suppose the greatest lesson I learned was times can change, folks can change, and love softens the hearts. With the gift of money I left behind, I'll continue to be a blessing to others.

If All Minds Are Clear

March 20, 1995

Chapter One

Nearing the conclusion of another spirit filled communion Sunday at Grace Baptist Church on a beautiful Spring day, Reverend Cousins stood, wiped the sweat from his face, smiled then exclaimed, " God is good!"

"All the time!" the congregation replied.

"And all the time!" Reverend Cousins bellowed.

" God is good!" we shouted back. Reverend Cousins is a bear of a man, a gentle giant if you will. His deep voice, firm handshakes, drooping eyelids and Christian warmth and kindness are what define him. Approaching the back end of his sixties, and slower now in both step and speech, he's the only pastor Grace Baptist Church has ever known.

Reverend Cousins said, "My Lord! Now before we dismiss, and if all minds are clear, I want to welcome back our very own Brantley Wilkerson II. God has delivered him back to us, safe and sound from seminary. And I'm told he's brought a friend home with him. Why don't you step up here son and say a few words."

I took to the podium and said, "Good afternoon church. First and foremost, I want to thank God for all of my blessings. I'm grateful to Him for blessing me to make it through seminary. Because without Him, and my friend Tucker here, I probably wouldn't have graduated. And since Tucker was unchurched, I invited him to come visit and see if he wants to join our family. Come on up here, Tucker, and introduce yourself to the congregation."

"Good afternoon, folks, I'm Tucker Wakefield, Brantley's friend, and like he said, we met at the seminary. You'll be proud to know, from the moment we met until now, all he talked about was Grace Baptist Church. He told me about how the Holy Spirit fills this house. He also told me about Reverend Cousins' powerful and moving sermons. He spoke about the kindness, caring and genuine Christian fellowship that's here. And from everything I've seen today, he undersold it. It's far better than I could have ever imagined! I lost my parents when I was five, and have no other family I know of. Family means everything to me, especially since I grew up in foster and group homes. So if you'll have me, I'd love to cast my lot with y'all and be a part of your family." The entire congregation stood and applauded as Reverend Cousins pulled Tucker into a bear hug and formally welcomed him into the fold. After the benediction, the congregation did the same. They were so moved by Tucker's speech, he received countless invitations for supper and lodging. But in the end, he decided to stay with me and my mother, Lois.

As the crowd dispersed, my fiancée', Viola, joined me. Beautiful, kind, and a bit naive, Viola is the Pastor and Ms. Annie's only child. Reverend Cousins is planning to retire at the year's end. And with the backing of the board of trustees, he'll appoint his successor before he leaves. Because I'm his son-in-law to be, I have the inside track. Our union has been forecasted by our parents since we were kids. And though I love and care about Viola dearly, I feel we lack the passion and chemistry necessary to sustain our union over the long haul. Nevertheless, I'll marry her still. I readily admit my wandering eye always holds sway to temptation's door. I have no doubt Viola's going to be an excellent wife and mother. In the meantime, I'll keep praying for God to deliver me from my transgressions, with the hope I can someday be the husband she deserves. I've yet to own up to or be called to the carpet for any of my mistakes. All my life, I've flown by the seat of my pants, relying on my charm and wit, along with others to see me through all of the trouble I've found myself in through the years.

After meeting and glad handling with the congregation, Tucker joined Viola and me in the vestibule near the main sanctuary's entrance. Since I hadn't introduced them yet, I believed now was the right time.

"Brantley, you were right, I love this church. The people here are so warm and kind, this is my home now," Tucker said.

"I'm so happy to hear that. Tucker, this is my fiancee', Ms. Viola Cousins."

"Pleased to meet you, Viola, it's an honor."

"Likewise, Tucker, the pleasure's all mine. Thank you for helping my baby make it through seminary," Viola replied.

"Oh, it was nothing, he did the work himself, I merely pointed out a few things for him here and there."

"Baby, don't let him fool you, he was a tremendous help," I said to Viola.

"Well, thank you just the same, Tucker, and welcome to our family."

"Thank you, Viola, I'm grateful to be here."

"Baby, I've got an idea. Since Mama and Daddy will be out visiting the sick and shut-in, why don't we eat out today?" Viola said.

"Ok, Sweetie, sounds good to me. How about you, Tucker, what do you say?"

"Sounds good, Bro, but I'll probably just accept one of the many supper invitations I received. Besides, you've been away for a while, go spend some quality time with your fiancee'. I'd just feel like a third wheel. Two's company, and three's a crowd you know."

Viola's eyes lit up the way they do when she's excited or has an idea. "Ooh, I know! What if I invite Jada to come with us? She's up in the office, why don't I go get her?"

"Ok, but remember what I said about matchmaking."

"Who's matchmaking, we're only going out for a bite to eat. It's not like they're going to meet and elope or something."

"Ok, go on and get her, I just don't want you starting in on Tucker. He hasn't even been here a whole day yet and you're already trying to marry him off."

"Aw, it's ok, Brantley, I don't mind. Besides, like Viola said, it's only supper."

And with that, Viola happily skipped down the hall to fetch her best friend.

Chapter Two

Minutes later, Viola and Jada came walking down the hallway giggling like a couple of schoolgirls. If there ever was an example of someone who's triumphed over tragedy, then Jada Sims is the poster child for it. With equal parts of beauty, intelligence, kindness, and grace, she's what the elders call an old soul and favored by God. Always upbeat with a positive attitude, she worked her way through college and grad school before founding her own accounting firm. Grace Baptist is just one of her many clients. Unattached, her only flaw to my knowledge is her inability to maintain a serious relationship. I'm sure her insecurities and trust issues with men have a lot to do with never knowing who her real father is. But, judging from the way she's ogling Tucker with a huge grin plastered on her face, and with him returning the same grin to her, maybe this meeting holds some promise. After all, they do have a lot in common. Both of them are highly motivated self-starters.

Still grinning, Viola stepped between Tucker and Jada and said, "Reverend Tucker Wakefield, please meet my best friend, Ms. Jada Sims."

Tucker stepped around Viola, extended his hand and said, "It is indeed an honor to make your acquaintance, Ms. Sims."

Shaking Tucker's hand, Jada returned Tucker's smile and said, "Likewise, Reverend Wakefield."

"Please, Ms. Sims, call me Tucker."

"Ok, Tucker, only if you call me Jada."

"It's a deal, Jada, forgive me for staring, but you're by far the prettiest woman I've met since I've been in Atlanta."

Giggling and clearly blushing, Jada replied, "Thanks for saying that, Tucker, but you're very handsome yourself."

"Wow, thanks, Jada!" beamed Tucker.

I stepped between them and playfully said, "Break it up folks, let's put this mushiness on hold for a little while, shall we? Because some of us here are ready to eat."

Tucker responded, "Ok, bud, we'll put it on hold for now, right, Jada?"

Jada smiled and said, "Ok, we'll stop for now because we can always pick it back up later."

"Sounds good, as long as it's a promise."

"It's a deal and a promise."

I looked at my watch and asked, "Can we go now?"

Dinner was amazing. Spectacular ambiance, and the food, drinks and conversation flowed. Tucker and Jada got along famously. So much so that by dessert, they were feeding each other. Afterwards, we stopped by this little out of the way nightspot for some jazz and drinks. Tucker and Jada carried on like they'd known each other for years. She sat in his lap at the table, and when they slow danced, their bodies were pressed together so tightly that from a distance they looked like one person. Between the kisses and whispers of sweet nothings to each other, they behaved as though they were the only people in the club. Needless to say, this pleased Viola to no end. I suppose I was happy for them as well, because they've both known and endured so much pain and loneliness in their lives. The last we saw of the lovebirds last night was them following each other out of the parking lot. Viola and I agreed not to pry into their business, but from all we've witnessed this evening, their coupling can only evolve to one conclusion.

Chapter Three

In the three and a half months that followed our dinner double date, Jada and Tucker's undying love for each other have them tee-
tering on the brink of matrimony. Their wedding is planned two Saturdays from now. To
say that the entire church is excited about their
nuptials would be an understatement. In the
short time he's been a part of our church family, Tucker has become indispensable and
beloved by all. Reverend Cousins will both offi-
ciate and give Jada away. He says he's always
seen Jada as a second daughter. I'm the best
man, and Viola is the maid of honor. And although Viola is thrilled about Jada's wedding,
she's planning for ours to be even bigger and
better than theirs. Another problem for Viola is
the fact that most folks can see the genuine
love, heat and passion between Jada and Tucker. To her, Tucker possesses the attributes
every man should possess: compassion, passion, sensitivity, thoughtfulness, attentiveness
and being romantic. I'll admit he's most things
I'm not. Not only me, but most of the menfolk
in the church. Most of all, it's his faithfulness
and fidelity that Jada, Viola and all of the
church's womenfolk value most. Of course it
doesn't help that I'm barely any of those things
to Viola. Nowadays, I find myself being constantly compared to Tucker. Don't get me

wrong, I love and respect Viola dearly, but just not in the way Tucker loves Jada. Marrying Viola will more or less get me to the place that my father and I always envisioned for me: to be the next pastor of Grace Baptist Church. Our marriage will be the culmination of a pact sworn long ago between my father and soon to be father-in-law, Reverend Cousins. I'm so close to realizing the dream that I can't allow no one or nothing to jeopardize it.

In the last days leading up to the wedding, Tucker's been a bundle of nervous energy. He and Jada are so looking forward to their wedding day, so much that neither one of them are able to contain themselves. They both want to start a family immediately. So does Viola, but not me. I'd much rather establish myself as pastor for a couple of years before even considering starting a family.

In addition to being head over heels in love with Jada, Tucker has fully immersed himself into the church. As our youth minister, he's created various ministries that have enthused the entire church. Membership among our youth has grown exponentially. He holds youth church during the regular worship service. He creates games and songs that help the kids learn more about the Bible. He's even talking about starting an after school tutoring and mentoring program. Here at Grace Baptist, he can do no wrong. If I didn't already have the inside track to being named Reverend Cousins' successor, and if Tucker wasn't such a great friend and brother to me, I'd be worried.

Last night, I threw Tucker an impromptu bachelor party. I rented a suite at one of the hotels downtown. I invited a few of the younger guys from church and some of the guys from seminary. Liquor flowed freely and endlessly. After the crowd thinned and Tucker passed out, I paid a couple of the dancers a little extra to undress him and pose for some provocative pictures. I hope I never have to use them, and I feel so guilty for stooping to such a level. But not so guilty to use them if I have to. Like my father used to say, "Plan for war in times of peace."

Chapter Four

Tucker and Jada's wedding day finally arrived, and Tucker was beside himself with joy; nervous, but incredibly happy and excited. According to Viola, so was Jada. During the ceremony, both tears and rejoicing were clearly evident. Even I shed a few, being in the midst of so much love and emotion, how could I not? Watching Tucker and Jada drive away, headed for their honeymoon, excited me a little about our wedding. I suppose I look forward to it because every pastor needs a great wife. I don't believe I can do any better than Viola. I know she loves me dearly, and will always faithfully support me and stand by my side. I've known her practically all my life. Besides my mom and Tucker, there's no one I trust more.

Before leaving the reception, I was cornered by Monica Hawkins. She is the daughter of Sister Ruby Hawkins, who chairs our board of trustees. Long widowed, she dotes on Monica and her son Robert and is fully immersed in their lives. If that wasn't enough, she constantly tries to marry her kids off because she's so desperate to be a grandmother. It's been long rumored that Robert is gay, so she tries all the harder to marry Monica off. She has no respect for my engagement to Viola. Since Viola's a virgin, Monica and I fool around from time to time. As far as I know, only Tucker, Monica and Mrs. Hawkins know I've deceived Viola. I suppose the only reason Sister Hawkins hasn't blackmailed me is the fact that she, Monica, and Robert would be publicly shamed and possibly exiled from the church. I know that aside from her kids, presiding over the board gives her the most joy. It fulfills her purpose. Plus, she knows I'm going to be named pastor soon, and she and I are going to need each other. My mother dislikes her a great deal because rumor has it she was just one of my father's many paramours.

Anyway, Monica suggested I meet her at her place after I take Viola home. I know I shouldn't have, but before long, I found myself at her apartment. It was a warm summer's night, and the black sky wore a full moon woven with a blanket of stars. Monica is a very attractive and sensual woman, so needless to say the sex is amazing. She claims her feelings run deep for me, and maybe they do, but she's a grown woman who knows I'm engaged to marry in less than a month. Plus, I'm a couple of weeks away from being named Reverend Cousins' successor. My mother hates and refuses to acknowledge this side of me because it reminds her of my father. I'm told he was a serial womanizer to the nth degree, and most of his lovers were members of Grace Baptist.

Chapter Five

A week and a half later, Tucker and Jada returned from their honeymoon more in love than ever. By this time, Viola, her mom, and my mom had finalized all of our wedding plans. All this week, from Sunday worship to Wednesday night Bible study, even to the Male Choir rehearsal on Friday evening, both Monica and Sister Hawkins have been trying to corner me. They told me they needed to speak with me in private as soon as possible. So, instead of risking being seen with them now, I told them to wait until rehearsal is over. That way, no one will see us, and we can talk while I lock the church up.

A heavy rain began to fall, lightning crackled in the sky along with occasional rumblings of thunder. They both glared at me with solemn looks. Sister Hawkins prodded Monica towards me and said, "Go on, tell him."

"Tell me what?" I asked.

Monica stared at the floor for a few seconds before saying, "I'm pregnant."

I looked at her sideways and asked, "What did you say?"

Sister Hawkins stepped in front of her and said, "You heard her, she's pregnant and the baby is yours! We want to know what you're going to do about it?"

They were both very upset. Sister Hawkins was now raising her voice, and tears were streaming down Monica's face.

"What do you mean, what am I going to do about it? What can I do? I'm supposed to be getting married next Saturday, and announced as the pastor's successor in two days! Why are you two springing this on me right now?"

Sister Hawkins, being a tall and fairly broad woman, stood directly face to face with me with flared nostrils and said, "My daughter is not some two bit whore you found on the street! You were engaged to be married every time you crawled between her legs! This time, I won't go away quietly! You better believe that!" The whole time Sister Hawkins was in my face, Monica was just standing there crying softly.

I looked over at her and asked, "What do you have to say about this?"

She wiped the tears from her face and said, "I am, and I've always been up front and honest about my feelings for you! You know I've been in love with you for some time now! Each time we've gotten together made me love you more! Yes, I'm pregnant, and yes, it's yours! Yes, I plan on keeping our child, and if you're the man of God you claim and put on to be when you stand in that pulpit, I expect you to do the right thing!"

"Which is?" I asked.

"Which is breaking it off with Viola Cousins and marrying my daughter!" Sister Hawkins interrupted, now screaming.

"You mean to say you're fine with all three of us being exiled from Grace Baptist?"

"No, what I'm saying is, as the Chairperson of the board of trustees, I have the power and enough votes to still make you pastor, even without the Pastor's backing. That is, as long as you do right by my child and make her your wife."

"How am I supposed to do that, the wedding's only a week away?"

"I don't know, and don't really care for that matter, but let me make it even simpler for you to understand. If you marry Viola, you'll never be pastor of Grace Baptist Church, I'll see to it your life becomes a living hell! But if you marry my Monica, I can give you what you've always wanted, and what your Daddy always wanted for you. Being a Pastor is about making tough decisions, and doing what's right in the eyes of God. If you choose to make the right choice, wait until Pastor appoints you, before you break it off with Viola." Staring at me squarely in the eye, I'll never forget her putting her hand on my shoulder and saying, "Please do the right thing, Brantley, please do right by my baby here. She and Robert are all I have in the world, along with your child she's carrying." And just like that, she and Monica were gone.

Gone, after leaving me with a lot to digest and think about.

Chapter Six

Sunday's worship was nearing its conclusion when Reverend Cousins stood and approached the podium. Still in the spirit from his sermon, he removed his glasses and wiped the sweat away from his chubby face. After tucking his handkerchief away, he smiled and said, "Brothers and sisters, if I may and if all minds are clear, I need to make an announcement before we adjourn. After the Lord helped Moses deliver the Israelites from Egypt's bondage, He caused them to wander because of their lack of faith and disobedience of His word. He then told Moses he would not see the promised land. Therefore, Joshua was chosen to lead in Moses's stead. I feel, I mean I know I've taken Grace Baptist as far as I can. I say this with a pure conscience and a clean heart. It's time for some new blood, some young leadership to take us into the twenty-first century that's rapidly approaching. Someone able and savvy enough to navigate the currents of technology so that Grace Baptist Church can continue to be that shining light on the hill serving our community. A Church that will continue to worship, serve and love the God we cannot see as well as our brothers and sisters we see every day. So without further ado, it's my privilege and honor to present to you Grace Baptist Church's next pastor, Brantley Wilkerson II."

I stood to raucous applause and a standing ovation. Reverend Cousins and Tucker squeezed me into bear hugs before I made it to the podium.

There were no words to describe how lousy and worthless I felt inside. There was no way I could accept this position. I know I've done some terrible and disgusting things in my lifetime, but this has to be the lowest I've ever stooped and felt.

I motioned for everyone to be seated, so I could speak. "Brothers and Sisters, I've waited all my life for this moment, but now that it's here, I cannot in good conscience accept this appointment."

Gasps and murmurs filled the congregation. Viola, Ms. Annie, my mom, Tucker and Jada were all shocked, wearing puzzled looks. Even Sister Hawkins and Monica were looking at me sideways.

I added, "I've been living a lie. I've been dishonest and deceitful for far too long."

Reverend Cousins looked at me and said, "What's the matter, son? Make it plain."

I cleared my throat and said, "I'm not worthy to shepherd this flock. I have shamed myself before the eyes of God. I've been sleeping with Monica Hawkins behind my fiancee's back, and now she's pregnant with my child."

I'll never forget the look of disgust and hurt on Viola's face. She walked as far as the altar, pointed her finger at me and angrily said, "I hate you, Brantley Wilkerson, and I never want to see you again." People were now pointing and shaking their heads in disgust. Sister Hawkins was furious with me, and Monica was sobbing. And the look of disgust and disappointment my mother gave me just cut me to the core - I felt terrible. Reverend Cousins tried to stand but collapsed. Tucker and I started CPR, but by the time the paramedics arrived, we'd lost him to the ages. Needless to say, by this time, Viola was beating on me and trying to revive her father at the same time.

Chapter Seven

Reverend Cousins' home going celebration was held the following Thursday on a beautiful, warm and sunny day. Naturally, I stayed away out of respect for Ms. Annie and Viola. I'm told the celebration had all of the pomp and dignity he deserved. He was like a father to me, and I feel I let him down. I'm told Tucker gave an amazing eulogy, and the service was very moving. Ministers and dignitaries from all over the city came to pay their respects. After the wake, the night before the home going, I waited until everyone left the funeral home to spend a few moments with Reverend Cousins' body. I felt I at least owed him that. Truth is, I owed him so much more. He was always so kind and helpful to me. He was my mentor and one of my biggest supporters. I pray he forgives me.

Aside from Mama, Tucker, and Jada, I had no contact or had heard from anyone from Grace Baptist. Tucker had been named Pastor of Grace Baptist, and I had no problem with that. In fact, I was happy for him. I knew I didn't deserve to be, besides, I knew in my heart with Tucker at the helm, Grace Baptist would thrive and prosper to higher and higher heights. They were in the best possible hands.

About a week later, I was awakened by the doorbell. Night had fallen, and of course, I was still feeling sorry for myself. Sorry, but relieved at the same time. For once, I stood up like a man and did the right thing. For the first time in my life, I didn't hide behind anyone or try to shift the blame elsewhere. For the first time since my father's been gone, I owned my mistake.

I was shocked when I opened the door and saw Ms. Annie standing there. She smiled and said, "Good evening, Brantley, may I come in? I need to speak to you for a minute." After letting her in, offering her a seat and something to drink, she smiled and said, "I want you to know that I don't blame you for Solomon's passing. It was just his time. I also want you to know I forgive you for what you did to my daughter. And I'm sure in time, Viola will also. I need to share a true story with you, but before I do so, promise me it'll go no further than this room."

"I promise, Ms. Annie."

"Ok, I'm going to hold you to that promise. Long ago, when Grace Baptist was just a dream that we were trying to build from the ground up, Solomon was away from home a lot. We'd just gotten married, and he'd preach at any church and revival that would have him. We needed the money. He was full of big ideas and longed for the day he'd pastor his own church. He, along with your father, convinced a group of folks to pool their money to buy this small church. Solomon was always gone somewhere with your father. At first, I was just lonely, then I resented the fact he was always gone.

Meanwhile, on Sundays, I had to smile, stand, cheer, keep up appearances and be the perfect first lady. So one night, with Solomon away and in a moment of weakness, I stepped outside of our marriage. An old friend from back home was in town, we went out for a drink, and the next thing I knew, I was pregnant with Viola. I felt so terrible, I had to tell Solomon. When I confessed, he was upset, but he forgave me. He knew in his heart he couldn't preach forgiveness if he wasn't willing to practice forgiveness himself. He said Viola was his, and he'd raise her as such. To this day, she doesn't know the truth. We agreed to never tell her. As you can see, that's exactly what he did. But before we turned in that night, he said he needed to tell me something also. He said one night when he was counseling Ella Sims, he had a moment of weakness and slept with her. Now at the time, Ella was one of my best friends. She could never look me in the face again. I suppose that's the reason she drank so much. That's probably what made Deacon Sims stray from home so much, and why he and Jada never shared a close bond. That's also why until Tucker came along, Jada always had trust issues with men. But now you see why Jada and Viola are so close to each other. They don't know the truth, and I pray they never will.

He also confessed to sleeping with Ruby Hawkins around the same time, and a child was produced from that union as well, Monica

Hawkins. But unlike Ella, Ruby was a hothead who threatened to out her and Solomon's secret to the whole congregation. Solomon and your father placated her by making her the chairperson of the board of trustees, carrying the note for her home and giving her a monthly stipend.

Your father was a wonderful man, he willingly gave one of his titles to Ruby just to appease her and keep the peace. He loved Solomon and Grace Baptist so much, he allowed the rumors of Solomon's sins to be his. He was never the man folks thought he was. He took the heat, and was even willing to sacrifice his reputation so that someday you'd be named Solomon's successor. That's how much he loved and believed in you. Over the years, each time Solomon fell to temptation, your father would take the blame for it. Now, I'm not nominating your father for sainthood, because as you can see, none of us are perfect. We are all flawed and have crosses to bear, but the key is to own our faults, work through them and hopefully, learn from them. I've forgiven you, but it's time you forgive yourself. Promise you'll do so, and keep my confidence. I just wanted you to know you're not the first person to make such a mistake, and you surely won't be the last. Good evening, son."

"Good evening, Ms. Annie, and thanks for coming by and making me feel better."

"You're very welcome. Solomon and I have always loved you like a son, and I always will."

"Thanks again, Ms. Annie." I felt a lot better after she left, freer and not as guilty. So after I prayed for a bit, and left everything in God's hands, I laid down and drifted off to sleep.

Chapter Eight

The next morning, right after Mama left for the grocery store, the doorbell rang. Monica and Sister Hawkins were at the door. When I answered, she said, "Good morning, Brantley, we'd like a word with you."

"Good morning yourselves. Sure, come in and have a seat. You just missed mama."

"I know, we waited for her to leave. We weren't exactly her favorite people before all of this happened, so you can imagine how she probably feels about us now."

"Mama's not like that, ma'am, besides, I'm all ears and anxious to hear what you have to say."

She stood, sighed and said, "First of all, that took a lot of guts for you to do what you did. We, along with at least fifty members were impressed, including five members of the trustee board. Now, we have no problem with Pastor Wakefield, and we'll always love Grace Baptist, but we're planning on starting a church of our own. I guess what I'm trying to say is, we need a pastor, and were wondering if you'd consider coming on board. I'm not here to put any pressure on you, you're a grown man and Monica is a grown woman. As of this moment, I'm out of y'all's business. You two have to work it out on your own. Whether you marry or not, you still have a child on its way to this world. So, think about it and let me know, ok?"

"Yes, ma'am, I'll do just that." Aside from saying hi and bye, Monica didn't say much of anything. I watched them leave, get into her Cadillac and drive off.

The following evening, after a haircut and shave, I made my way over to the Hawkins household. It was another beautiful summer night replete with twinkling stars and a full moon in the sky. In the weeks following Reverend Cousins' passing, I've had a lot to think about and process. But what's crystal clear to me now is the fact that I must finally grow up and be a man accountable for my actions. I also discovered that not being a pastor isn't the end of the world. We're all human and surely fall short of God's glory. We're not perfect, nor will we ever be. All we can do when we fall and make a mistake is to seek God's forgiveness, forgive ourselves and learn from them.

When I rang the doorbell, Monica answered the door. She looked really good, she was glowing as a matter of fact. Although we made some mistakes together, I believe in my heart our unborn child is not one of them. It's a gift from God, and He never makes any mistakes. After greeting each other, I asked her if I could come in. She said yes, and said she'd go get her mother.

I put my hand on her shoulder and said, "Wait a minute, I want to talk to you first." She took her seat, with a surprised look on her face. I sat beside her, looked her in the eyes and said, "Look, I know we're equally responsible for what happened. And while we didn't plan on having a child together, the fact remains that we are having a child together. An innocent child, a gift from God who needs both its mother and father." I knelt before her, took her hand and said, "I don't have much to offer right now, I don't even have a job. I can't even afford a ring, but I want to do right by you and our child. So, if you'll have me, I'd love for you to be my wife. Will you marry me?"

She stood, covered her mouth with her hands, smiled and screamed, "Yes, nothing will make me happier than to be your wife and a mother to your children!"

Sister Hawkins entered the living room and asked, "What's going on in here?"

We looked at each other, laughed and I said, "We're getting married, I want to do right by Monica and our child. And if the offer still stands, I accept, I'll be honored to be your pastor, besides, I really need a job right now. I have a family to support."

We eloped to Las Vegas the next day. Sister Hawkins, or Mama Ruby as I now called her, gave us quite the wedding present; enough money to take this trip, buy wedding bands and put the rest away. She and mama even made peace for our sakes. I moved in with Monica, and so began our journey as husband and wife.

A couple of years later, I ran into Viola at the grocery store. Not only did she forgive me, but she also congratulated me on my marriage and for being honest with her before it was too late. She's now happily married with two kids herself. I suppose God has His ways of making us all grow up and be accountable. We'll never be perfect, but we can always be better. Looking back, I can honestly say I'm a better man because of it. Daddy used to tell me that someday I'd have to stand on my own and right my wrongs. I learned it's not who falls, but who's willing to get back up. Now, I'm able to face and shepherd my flock as a pastor with both a clear mind and conscience.

Home

January 21, 2014

Chapter One

The same nightmare has roused me from my sleep for the past thirty years. Several traumatic events seem to have coiled themselves into the serpent in my mind that invades my nights with the frequency of my own breathing. I lost my beautiful mother to cancer when I was fifteen, and my younger brother Rudolph eight years before that after being hit by a car. My older sister, Juanita, left home in the middle of the night right after Mama died, and I haven't heard from her since. But the event that changed me forever and plagues my sleep occurred during the wee hours of a warm May morning. After graduating from high school hours earlier with a full academic scholarship to Morehouse College, my father, Paul Spires or Big Paul as he was known around Tutweiler, was always a binge drinker, but he'd been rapidly spiraling out of control since we lost Mama. I've heard Grandma say more than once that I was a product of rape, and out of fear of my Grandpa and my uncles, he married my underage Mama. Though she never did anything wrong to warrant Big Paul's physical and verbal abuse, I'm sure the weight of it all drove her to an early grave. I was born an albino, and because of false rumors and innuendo that's festered around town about my appearance since I've been born, he believed more and more that I wasn't his. I suppose on that night his ignorance and alcoholism had finally brought him to his boiling point, and he exploded in kind.

"Get your sorry ass out of bed, get all of your shit and get out of my house! I don't ever want to see your piss colored ass again! I've held my peace long enough, you, your ma, and her folks have made a fool out of me for the last time! I don't care no more!"

Still drowsy, I stumbled out of bed, grabbed a couple of trash bags and threw all my belongings in them. I got out of there as fast as I could before things got out of hand. He had a lot of pistols and usually carried one on him at all times. I vividly remember the crazed look he had on his face as he stepped aside so I could go out of the door past him, along with the shove to the back of my head. The last thing he said to me was, "If you ever come back to

Tutweiler, I'll kill you where you stand!" As far as I was concerned, that was something he'd never have to worry about.

It pains me to relive it so often, and because of this, I'm usually up for a while at night. At times, I never even manage to get back to sleep. Of course, I suppose it's all a matter of perspective. I also credit that horrific morning with further fueling my maniacal drive, focus and work ethic. Besides haunting me, it also helped me graduate from Morehouse as valedictorian, and do the same at Oxford.

It was at Oxford that I fell in love and married Heather McCaskey, the daughter of one of the wealthiest men in England, Rolf McCaskey. There, he and my mother-in-law, Olivia, saw past my race and unique appearance and didn't treat me like a novelty. Their only daughter's happiness was all that mattered. With my incredible drive and a small loan from my father-in-law, I've built the largest securities and brokerage firm in Seattle and all of the West coast.

I'm P. Randall Spires, from Tutweiler, Mississippi. It's a small town about seventy miles from Memphis, Tennessee and about one hundred forty miles from Jackson. It's three A.M. now, and as usual, I'm pacing the floor in my study wound tighter than a tennis ball. Unfortunately, Heather and her family don't know much about my family, other than what

I've told them. But to be honest, neither do I. Like I said, I haven't had any contact with my father, sister or anyone from back home. And the closest I've been to Mississippi since I left was Atlanta, and that was only during a layover for a flight. But all that changed when the phone rang.

Chapter Two

I heard Heather answering it. "Hello," she said, yawning.

"Who? I'm sorry, no one by that name lives here, I'm afraid I don't know a Little Paul, at least one that lives here. Oh, wait, you say he's your uncle from Tutweiler, and you're Rudolph, his sister Juanita's son. Hold on please." A nephew calling me at four a.m. out of the blue? Especially one that I don't know or have never spoken to.

It has to be something about my sister, I hope everything's ok.

I collected the phone from Heather and said, "Hello."

"Hello, Uncle Paul, I'm your nephew Rudolph. I'm sorry for waking you, I forgot about the time difference."

"It's ok, Rudolph, I happened to be up anyway. Is everything ok? How's your mother?"

"She's good, as a matter of fact, she's the reason I'm calling. Mama's turning fifty in a couple of weeks, and we're giving her a surprise birthday party. She talks about you all the time, and I was just wondering, just hoping you and your wife will join us. She'd really like to see you, and honestly, me, my sister, brother, and dad would also. I understand your thirtieth class reunion also coincides with this weekend.

Please come, or at least think about it. Like I said, we all would like to have you guys here with us. I can either drop you an invitation in the mail, or e-mail you all of the particulars." Even though I've never met Rudolph, I felt his warmth and kindness through the phone. And, for the first time in a long time, I felt no apprehension in my heart about finally returning home. Besides, family is family and home is home. I miss my sister, and look forward to meeting my niece, nephews and brother-in-law, and I'm also looking forward to all of them finally meeting Heather. It's been far too long. I'm even going to see my father. With him having dementia and living in an assisted living facility, I'm not sure he'll even remember me. Besides, healing won't take place, nor will closure, without forgiveness. Who knows? Maybe my haunting nightmares will finally cease.

"Grab a pen, Rudolph, and I'll give you our address."

"Great, Uncle Paul, give me a sec. Mama's going to be so surprised, and I speak for the rest of us when I say we all look forward to finally meeting you."

"We look forward to meeting all of you as well. I can't wait to see my big sister!"

"Neither can she, Uncle Paul; neither can she, trust me. This is going to be her best birthday ever."

"Well, that sounds wonderful, Rudolph. Give me your contact information and I'll e-mail you our itinerary."

"Ok, Uncle Paul," he replied. "Uncle Paul?"

"Yes, Rudolph, is there anything else?"

"It's just that everyone calls me Rudy."

"Ok, Rudy, only if you call me Paul."

"I'll do that, but only when you say it's ok to do so in front of mom. We're adults, but she still expects us to respect our elders."

"Point taken. I understand. Until we meet then?"

"Until we meet, Uncle Paul, bye now."

"Bye, Rudy."

Chapter Three

Before I could cradle the phone, Heather joined me in the family room with a concerned look on her face. "Is everything ok, love?" she asked.

"Yes, sweetheart, as a matter of fact, it is. That guy on the phone was my nephew, Rudy, Juanita's son."

"Your sister Juanita?"

"Yes, the very same."

"Well, what did he want? Judging by that huge grin of yours, it must be good news of some sort."

"It is. They're throwing Juanita a surprise fiftieth birthday party, and they want us to attend. I told him we would; do you think we should go?"

"Absolutely! You and your sister haven't seen or spoken to each other in thirty years. Far too long if you ask me. I can't imagine what it's been like for both of you.

You need to do this Randy, both of you. You even need to see your father as well. I believe and I know it'll do you both a world of good. I'm sure your therapist would agree. Maybe you'll find closure, or at least gain enough peace within to bring an end to the nightmares. I'm no therapist, but even I know the pain from the past remains until we gain the courage to face and work through it. When is the party?"

"Two Saturdays from now."

"Your class reunion invitation came in the mail. It's scheduled for the same weekend. I'll call, RSVP and make our flight arrangements now."

"Don't you mean later this morning, sweetie?"

"I mean right now, love. I'm far too excited to sleep. I have a good feeling about this Randy. You, me, Randy and Mia, we all need this. I know they can't get away from school right now, but hopefully, they'll have a chance to meet and get to know them in the future. There's a whole side of their family they've yet to know."

"Sounds good, honey, but let's just take one step at a time, ok?"

"You're right love, let's do that. Come to bed now."

"I'm too wound up to sleep now, babe."

She took me by the hand, smiled seductively, and said, "Exactly, I didn't say anything about sleep, now, did I?"

Chapter Four

As the plane descended into Jackson, I took a few deep breaths, looked out of the window and took in as much of the city as I could. Along with my lingering anxiety, thoughts, memories, and feelings flooded through me as we landed. Tutweiler is only about one hundred and forty miles away. The seventeen year old boy who was forced to leave there in the middle of the night returns as a successful forty-seven year old who is hoping to once and for all heal some old wounds and finally rid himself of the demons he's carried inside him ever since.

I think about my mother often and try to imagine what my life would be like if she was still here. She was my bedrock, my biggest supporter and best friend all rolled up into one. Juanita ran a close second. I have some guilt about not being in contact with her all of these years, and I'm sure she does also. But holding on to the pain and disappointment of our pasts will only hold us there. Resolving them will bring us both present with hopes of a brighter future.

Mama raised me to love myself unconditionally and to be more proud of how I see myself rather than how the world saw me. She always said God made me extra special for a reason and someday I'll know what that reason is. She told me to never allow folks on the outside to take away all of the goodness and power I have inside. Still, I regret it's taken me this long to get the nerve to come back here. Problems don't resolve themselves I suppose, and hopefully, before this trip is over, I'll accomplish that. But it won't happen without me accepting some of the responsibility myself.

After picking up our luggage and grabbing our rental car, Heather and I left the airport headed downtown for our hotel. It was a beautiful and warm summer day. I'd almost forgotten how beautiful Mississippi can be this time of the year. Needless to say, having never seen the south, Heather was beyond excited, and I must admit, so was I. So after phoning Rudolph and freshening up a bit, we headed to the restaurant to meet and dine with Rudolph, Paul, Rachel and their spouses.

Chapter Five

We all recognized each other immediately when we saw each other. Of course, Heather and I weren't too hard to pick out, but surprisingly, neither were my niece and nephews. Rachel was the spitting image of mama, Rudolph looked exactly like my little brother and there was even a strong resemblance between Paul and I. Dinner was amazing. It went better than I could have ever imagined. Besides sharing a wonderful meal and a couple of bottles of the best wine, they caught us up on their lives and we did the same. They shared pictures, and so did we. They told us all about their parents, Juanita and Robert. They met and retired in the Air Force, where Juanita earned her GED, Bachelor and Master's degrees while serving as a registered nurse. And upon retiring, she took a job at Memorial Hospital and worked another ten years. Robert, her husband served as a fireman in the Air Force and worked as an arson investigator for the JFD for another fifteen years. After saying our goodbyes, Heather and I drove back to the hotel and went for a little stroll to work off the dinner, dessert, and wine. I felt really, really good and was excited about finally reuniting with my sister tomorrow at her party. I'm sure we are both going to be speechless. If I have any difficulty sleeping tonight, it won't be because of the nightmare, it will be because of my excitement.

Chapter Six

Despite my enthusiasm, I slept pretty well. And I must admit that in this past couple of days, Heather and I have been making love like we did in college. It's ended our nights and started our days.

During breakfast, I thought it would be a good idea to finally visit my father. His permanent care facility is here in Jackson, and not too far from downtown. I have no expectations about this visit, only optimism and hope. I needed to see him. I can honestly say I have no hatred and anger in my heart for him. Whether he regretted it or not, it was up to me to forgive him. Not for him, but for me, I felt it was very necessary. The kids told me last night his dementia is rapidly progressing. There were only flashes and glimpses of him remembering anything at all.

The facility was very nice. Of course, I already knew this because I pay for it. The staff was friendly and accommodating and really exercised the utmost of care and patience with the patients. Heather and I were impressed, this was a first class facility, worth every penny.

When we entered his room, he was sitting in his wheelchair watching the weather channel. We were told that aside from watching CNN sometimes, the weather channel is all he watches. He was a great deal smaller than I remembered, bald but neatly dressed and groomed wearing a pressed shirt, pair of khaki slacks and some slippers. When a commercial came on, he turned towards us, smiled and said, "How are y'all doing? It's a beautiful day out there today, isn't it? The weatherman here says it's going to be like this all week." Motioning towards his bed, he said, "Have a seat, take a load off. Have we ever met before? My mind just comes and goes sometimes."

I felt my eyes water, looked at Heather and said to him, "I'm Paul, your son, and this is my wife, Heather."

He gave me a puzzled look, extended his hand and said, "Good to meet you, young fellow. You sure have a pretty wife there. Pleased to meet you too, young lady."

"I'm honored to meet you as well, sir. How are you feeling today?"

"I'm blessed to still be above the ground, and that's good enough for me. God is good."

"Indeed He is, sir, all the time."

Aside from some small talk going both ways, he gave us both puzzling looks, me especially. After a couple of hours, we asked him if he'd like to go out with us for lunch. Surprisingly, he asked for a raincheck because today was meatloaf day, his favorite. When lunchtime came, he asked us if we would come visit him again. I told him we would. As we stood to leave, he grabbed Heather's hand and said, "Can I have a hug, young lady?"

Sniffling, Heather said, "Of course, you can, Dad, I thought you'd never ask."

Next, he looked at me and said, "How about you, young fella, can I get a hug from you, too?"

Before he could even get it all out, I jumped up, grabbed him, hugged him and sobbed. I squeezed him so tightly, my watch fell off my wrist. The feeling was indescribable, I literally felt decades of anxiety dissipating. I must have held him for a couple of minutes before he said, "Are y'all coming tomorrow to see me?"

"We sure are," said Heather, "count on it."

"Good, well, be safe out there, I heard people drive real crazy these days."

Laughing, I said, "We will, Dad, don't worry, we'll see you tomorrow."

Heather drove us back to the hotel. We were both crying, but I was bawling too hard to see the road.

It was a happy cry, though. If I'm feeling this way today, I can't even begin to imagine what tonight's going to be like when I finally see Juanita. Afterwards, we drove to Tutweiler. The birthplace of blues music, it was still quaint and seemed a lot smaller than I remembered. We placed some flowers on my mama's and Rudolph's grave and said a prayer for them both.

Chapter Seven

Ever since we left our visit with dad, Heather and I were both filled with the highest joy and excitement. But now, on our drive over to the party venue, I felt as though I was going to burst inside. We've been all over the world, and we both agree that for obvious reasons, this has been the greatest vacation we've ever had. I couldn't be happier with how everything's turned out.

Parking the car and walking inside, we could hear the music blaring and people laughing and talking. We were received warmly and introduced to everyone at the same time by Rudolph. He told us that though the secret's out of the bag about the party, Heather and I being there was still going to be a huge surprise. He said his Dad was going to call when they were on their way. Moments later, he led us to a room with food and drinks to wait until he came for us.

About a half hour after we heard them singing happy birthday, we heard the DJ ask Juanita to come to the stage for a special presentation. Rudy came and led us to the rear of the stage. When the DJ told her to turn around, it was like time stopped for a few minutes. We both stood and stared at each other for what seemed like the longest time before she removed her hands from over her mouth and said, "Paul! My God, is that you?"

I couldn't even get audible sound to leave my mouth, I couldn't speak. She ran, screamed and jumped into my arms. We both stood there weeping and holding each other for the longest time. I noticed a lot of the people there were crying as well. I stepped back, looked her in the eyes and said, "Yes, Sis, it's me. Happy Birthday! You don't know how much I missed you!"

"Yes, I do, I missed you just as much! I hate that we've missed thirty years of our life together!"

"I do too, but you know what, the past is in the past, this is now going forward. Let's vow to make the rest of our days the best. I went to see Dad today, and it made me feel real good. Oh, where are my manners! Heather, come meet my big sister!"

Heather, wiping away tears squeezed Juanita into a bear hug and said, "Pleased to meet you, Juanita."

"Pleased to meet you, Heather. Thank you so very much for taking good care of my little brother."

"Believe me, the pleasure's been all mine!"

"Robert, get over here and meet my brother!" Robert walked over, introduced himself and hugged me as well.

The next night, Heather and I attended my class reunion and shared another great evening laughing, dancing and fellowshipping with my old classmates. Here, reuniting with the class of 1984, I was just Paul. Introducing Heather, reintroducing myself and forging new bonds. The next day, we all got together and had a huge family dinner. We promised to come back when the kids were out of school and invited them to come to Seattle to visit us. Nightmares can end, old wounds can heal, peace can replace the pain of the past, and you can go home again.

Heather and I were so happy, we decided we'd find a home in Jackson where we could live whenever we visited. As our plane climbed into the clouds taking us back to Seattle, I was more than happy to leave the nightmares where they first began.

A Balanced Imbalance

May 30, 2008

Chapter One

Frantic voices shook, prodded and lifted me from my bed onto a gurney. Barely conscious, dazed with my head spinning, I heard someone say, "He has a pulse, hurry. Bring those pill bottles so we'll know what he's ingested. From the looks of it, he washed the pills down with this rum. Hurry, get him in the ambulance and down to the emergency room."

I couldn't speak, but I wanted so badly to say, "Please leave me be and just let me go. I'm nothing, I have no real friends or family to speak of. No one to love and no one to love me. My life isn't capable of holding happiness or joy. I'm tired of riding this emotional roller coaster, wearing this fake mask of happiness and hiding my true self, day after day. I just want the pain to end, I'm a shell, with my mind in a thick haze. I'm totally hollow inside, unable to escape the dark shadows and barely existing."

At nineteen, I was diagnosed with Bipolar Disorder II, and ever since I've cycled from the heights of mania to the far depths of depression where I now find myself. More often than not, it's hereditary. Years of therapy unearthed the trauma of me coming home from school in the third grade and finding my mother dead from a self-inflicted gunshot wound. Of the two poles, my manic state feels indescribably amazing. During those times, I felt invincible, God-like and incredibly creative. My thoughts race so fast I can't seem to hold onto one. The only downside to mania is the reckless spending, hallucinating, promiscuity, lack of sleep and decreased appetite. The periods of mania don't last, and it's also an extremely dangerous state with a deep and dark depression to follow. That's what I dread and hate the most. Its effects can linger on for years. I barely have the energy to get out of bed. It's when I feel locked in a powerful vacuum of hopelessness and despair, like I've fallen in a deep, dark hole. A hole with a rope ladder anchored from the outside in. It feels like no matter how many rungs I climb, I can never escape before the walls close in and smother me. I've tried every form of treatment available, even ECT, but the demons of darkness lying in the shadows emerge and slowly overtake me. I suppose I'm to blame also, since I don't always follow my psychiatrist's advice. I don't take my meds every day and I occasionally miss appointments - don't always exercise or eat right either. I suppose the simple truth is, I'm thirty-five now and I'm just tired. I have nothing left. Obviously, this attempt failed, but prayerfully the next one won't.

Chapter Two

On the surface, those who know or have heard of me would think my life was perfect and I have everything to live for. I'm Zachary Price, aka DJ Zach of Zach in the A.M. fame. I host the number one syndicated radio show in the nation. I also co-host a local TV show, promote parties, work the best clubs in Atlanta, and run my own charitable foundation. I'm set for life financially, and loaded with all of the material wealth anyone could ever want or need. I'm in the who's who of Atlanta and one of its most eligible bachelors to boot. But on the inside, where true happiness and real treasure lies, I'm completely empty; tapped out. With every passing moment, it feels like the hole grows darker and deeper. So much so that no hospital, meds, or group therapy can ever come close to healing me.

At the hospital, after my stomach's been pumped and I'm stabilized, I'll be moved upstairs to the psych ward. Normally, it's only a seventy-two hour observation, but suicide attempts indicate an intent to harm one's self. Prior to this attempt, I'm usually escorted in shackles to the psych ward under an assumed name. Freedom and decision making for myself will be taken away. I'll say whatever I have to say, and do whatever I must do to get out of here. I'm unsure how the police even knew to come to my home to check on me, but I suspect my assistant Stephanie called them. She's Gail's sister, my show's producer. They're both very protective of me and I can always count on their loyalty and discretion. Truth is, I don't deserve them, they're the closest thing I've ever had to family. My shows and other businesses can take care of themselves. I've always been fortunate to have great people around me. I just don't feel worthy of it.

After reluctantly signing the admission papers, my psychiatrist, Dr. Joshua Lucas, paid me a visit. I feel guilty because I really like him. Along with the group and individual therapy, he'll try different meds with me to see which ones work best. The most successful one was lithium, but I was on it for so long it began to affect my kidneys. I took so much that at times I felt like a battery. And since I see only one way out of my darkness and despair, I'll take my time and be patient; I won't even try to escape. I'll just end the pain for good once I'm released.

Chapter Three

After a month and a half of intensive treatment and therapy, I was discharged and taken back home. Fortunately, it was Summer and the ruse of a vacation covered for me. I normally don't schedule that much this time of year anyway. Physically, I have no energy or appetite and sleep is very scarce. Down twenty-five pounds and rapidly weakening, I can barely muster enough energy to pull the covers away, get out of the bed and use the bathroom. My appearance is horrific -I haven't had a haircut or shave in weeks. Barely showering, brushing my teeth or even combing my hair. I'm taking my meds as prescribed, though I continue to free fall, moment by moment. Stephanie and Gail have been wonderful as usual. They take care of me and protect me. Besides them, Dr. Lucas and his staff, no one else knows my condition; which in and of itself has probably worsened my condition. It heightens the stress of being who I truly am and wearing the "my life is together" mask in public. In bed, surveying my bedroom, I look at my chair and wonder how much energy it'd take to grab a belt and hang from my pull up bar. There's a huge gulf between wishing death to take me and actually doing it myself. I was readying myself to get out of bed when the phone rang. The caller ID let me know Dr.

Lucas was calling again, probably to check on me.

"Hi, Zach, how are you feeling today?"

"Hi, Doc, nothing's changed much. Feels like the hole is growing deeper and darker."

"Please try to eat, and get a little rest, ok?

"Ok, I doubt it'll make me feel any better."

"Look, Can you do me a favor, please?

"Sure, what is it?"

"I need you to do a couple of things for me, ok?"

"I'm listening."

"I want you to shave, shower, eat, get a haircut, put on some clean clothes and come see me in the morning, Ok?"

"OK, Doc, what time?"

"See you at ten A.M?"

" That's way too early, It's gonna take some time for me to do that. How about two o'clock?"

"Perfect. I want you to come in with an open mind, I have some things I'd like to discuss."

"Ok, I'll be there, goodbye."

I arrived at Dr. Lucas' office about ten minutes shy of two P.M. A couple of minutes later, he entered the waiting area and escorted me to his office. Now seated, he said, "So Zach, how's it going? How are you coping?"

"I'm not, Doc. I feel like I'm sinking further down into a bottomless pit. I have no energy, I barely eat and sleep and my quality of life sucks. Why'd you want to see me today?"

"I'd like a commitment and a favor from you."

"Ok, what is it?"

"First, I need you to really dig in and give me and the treatment a chance. I know it doesn't feel like it now, but your life has both purpose and meaning. I just want you to try as hard as you possibly can. Do you think you can do that?"

"I'm willing to commit and do everything I possibly can to escape this darkness. What's the favor you need from me?"

"Well, first off I believe part of your struggle has been your lack of commitment, but the other part is the undue stress and energy it takes to conceal your condition. I told you at the beginning that it doesn't have to be a death sentence nor will it stop you from thriving and living a productive life because you've done it before. I want to take you to a treatment facility to spend some time with some adolescents. They look up to you and I believe this can be a great thing for them and you. But I don't want you to answer me now, go home and think about what I've said, ok?"

"Will do, I'll call you in a couple of days. I promise to commit and try to do what you've asked of me."

"Ok, that's all I ask. Enjoy the rest of your day."

"You do the same."

Chapter Four

I spent the rest of the day in bed thinking about what Doctor Lucas discussed with me. To be fair, I've never given myself a chance to try to get the consistent quality of life I've sought since my diagnosis. What could it hurt to take my meds every day, eat decently, exercise and get the proper amount of rest? The journey will no doubt be challenging and surely won't be quick, but if I chip away a little at a time, it's possible to eventually shed the darkness.

About a month later, Dr. Lucas drove me up to Briar Peace. It's a treatment facility for adolescents dealing with all types of mental illness, including bulimia, self-mutilation, ADD, CPD, schizophrenia and so on. On the drive up, he explained to me that although some of the kids have had multiple admissions, they're determined to face and survive their diagnoses.

My spirits were lifted when I was introduced to speak to the kids. Even facing their own demons, I was warmly welcomed. They were genuinely excited to see me. It felt pretty good to be surrounded by so much positive energy, and around people I can relate to, even if they're younger. After promising them I'd be back real soon, I left there feeling a little better. I suppose being with folks I can truly relate to had something to do with it. It definitely made me not feel so sorry for myself.

Obviously, Dr. Lucas is on to something here. What's now clear to me is that the stigma, fear, and shame I've held onto all these years kept me cloaked in darkness and despair. But if I am to climb out of the hole that imprisons me and scale the highest mountain, I must rid myself of fear and no longer hide.

After a relatively peaceful night's sleep, I woke up excited just thinking about yesterday's meeting with and speaking to those young adults. For the first time in a very long time, I was hopeful and determined to embrace life to the fullest.

Chapter Five

Dr. Lucas was right, by following his instructions to the letter, slowly and surely, I began to feel better. Attending group therapy with my peers and visits with the adolescents have done a world of good for me. My meds have been re-calibrated, I'm back in the gym and I'm definitely eating and sleeping better. Negotiations for my new contract are underway, and my non-profit is really thriving. Our annual back to school supply drive is coming up, and I look forward to being more involved with that.

The following week, my agent called and told me the station's brass wanted to meet with me to finalize the new deal. In the past, I've never disclosed my condition, but I'm tired of all the stress that comes with hiding it, so I've decided to tell them. Seated in the conference room with the executives, and after agreeing to terms, I asked for a moment to say a word or two before signing. "First, I want to thank you for your support of all my ideas and myself in general. I immensely enjoy our relationship. I just want to say before I sign this that I've kept a huge part of who I am to myself. I was diagnosed with Bipolar Affective Disorder II at the age of nineteen and have lived with it ever since. Until now, I've always seen it as a personal matter, but the truth is I've never felt better since I've been telling people about it." I could tell by reading some of the faces as I spoke that some of them were a little uneasy about what I said.

Jason Beck, the program director, stood and said, "Thank you for sharing that with us, Zach, I know this wasn't an easy decision for you - I'm proud of you. Ladies and gentlemen of the board, do you have any questions or concerns?"

Stuart Netter, the vice president, looked at me and said, "I think I speak for everyone present when I say that we too are grateful for you being so forthcoming with us, especially when you didn't have to. We're equally proud as well. We have a great thing going here, you've had the number one rated show in Atlanta for more than ten years. We want nothing more than for that to continue, but would you have a problem not disclosing your condition on air?" I was stunned. Here I was suffering in silence, hiding my condition, fearing they'd let me go because of it. But when I tell them, they don't want me to mention it on air. I stood with my hands on top of my chair and asked, "Why would you have a problem with me disclosing it? I've just explained to you all how much better I feel since I'm no longer hiding it. Besides, I'm not ashamed - I know there are others out there like I once was; cowering, suffering in silence and at the end of their rope. I'm afraid this is a deal breaker for me, I have to stay true to myself. I want to be more hands-on in the community with my non-profit now anyway. I've thoroughly enjoyed speaking and meeting with adolescents and adults alike struggling with mental illnesses. I know I can make a difference. I've enjoyed my time here, and I'll take all of the great memories created here. So let's part ways amicably, shall we?"

Everyone in the room, including my agent, were looking around at each other shocked.

Jason stood and said, "It sounds like your mind's made up, we wish you only the highest and best going forward. Just remember the non-compete clause kicks in immediately. Godspeed friend."

"Thanks, Jason, and thanks to all of you. Be blessed!"

Chapter Six

I left the offices and never looked back. A couple of days later, on my TV show, I disclosed my condition. I can't put into words how liberating that felt. Surprisingly, the network execs reached out to me and offered me a spot on a national morning TV show. Of course, I had to wait a year before actually appearing on air. I also drastically cut back on my club gigs.

The bulk of my time was spent working with those living with mental illnesses, especially young folks. It has been the most rewarding thing I've ever done in my life. There was a time I would never have believed that my life could be filled with so much joy and peace. Releasing the hidden darkness, secrecy and shame that lurked within propelled me back to the outside world. I'll still have obstacles in my path to negotiate and hills to climb, but I'll never have to do it in secret, ever again. Even if I'm unable to ever overcome my demons, I possess the faith to face them head on. I'm a new person, I travel all over the country speaking and meeting with those who struggle daily, hoping to transform lives. I've been blessed and I hope I'll be a blessing to others. Faith and trust in God do move mountains; I am a living example - through my imbalance, I have found the balance that I was missing!

For more information about the author, go
to www.charlesrbuttsjr.com

He can also be reached on,

Twitter: @Charlesrbuttsjr.com

Instagram: charlesr.butts, and

Facebook: Charles R. Butts Jr.